Joe and Sparky
Go to School

Joe and Sparky Go to School

Jamie Michalak

illustrated by

Frank Remkiewicz

CANDLEWICK PRESS

For Joan Powers,
and with special thanks to the stars of Sowams School
J. M.

For Sarah
F. R.

Text copyright © 2013 by Jamie Michalak
Illustrations copyright © 2013 by Frank Remkiewicz

First paperback edition 2014

Library of Congress Catalog Card Number 2012943657
ISBN 978-0-7636-6278-3 (hardcover)
ISBN 978-0-7636-7181-5 (paperback)

14 15 16 17 18 19 CCP 10 9 8 7 6 5 4 3 2 1
Printed in Shenzhen, Guangdong, China

This book was typeset in Adobe Caslon.
The illustrations were done in watercolor and colored pencil.

Candlewick Press
99 Dover Street
Somerville, Massachusetts 02144

visit us at www.candlewick.com

Contents

CHAPTER ONE
The Bus Ride

In Safari Land, the famous cageless zoo, a turtle hid in his shell.

Not far away, a giraffe stretched his neck to see the world.

"Look, Sparky!" said Joe Giraffe. "What is that?"

"Hmm," said Sparky. "It is big, yellow, and LOUD. It reminds me of somebody I know."

Joe read its side. "It is a SCHOOL BUS."

"What kind of bus is that?" asked
Sparky.

"Well," said Joe, "from the looks of it,
it is a bus for noisy short people."

The noisy short people got on the bus.
Then the bus headed toward Joe and
Sparky. It stopped right in front of them.

"Class, do not feed the animals!" said a lady on the bus.

"We will take a closer look," said Joe.

"No way, José!" said Sparky. "Every time you take a closer look at something, we get into trouble. I do not want trouble. I want a nap on my warm rock."

But Joe peeped into a window.

"AHHH!" yelled the short people.

"AGH!" yelled Sparky. He hid in his shell.

The short people laughed.

"Warm rock," Sparky squeaked.
"NOW!"

"But we have not seen the whole bus
yet," said Joe.

Joe pressed his face against a window.
He greeted the bus driver. He tested the
roof. *BANG, THUD, BANG!*

"I have seen enough!" yelled Sparky. He stepped off Joe's head. "Joe, bring me back to my pond!"

"OK, Sparky. Just one more min—"

VROOOM! The bus took off.

"The bus is going away," said Joe.

"I AM STILL ON THE BUS!" cried Sparky.

Joe watched Sparky grow smaller and smaller. He looked like a pea.

"SLOW DOWN, BUS!" yelled Sparky the pea. "SAFETY FIRST!"

"Do not worry, my small, green friend!" called Joe. "I will save you!"

Joe was no slowpoke. He caught the bus. He held on tight.

Joe and Sparky rode the bus out of the zoo,

Chapter Two
The Field Trip

The bus parked at a building. Joe stepped off the bus. He looked on top. All he saw was a dirty clump of leaves and bugs.

"Uh-oh. Where is Sparky?" Joe was worried.

Slowly, a small, scowling head poked out of the clump. "And this is why turtles do NOT ride buses!" it said.

"Sparky! It is you!" said Joe.

Sparky climbed onto Joe's head. "Where are we?"

"I do not know," said Joe.

The noisy short people got off the bus. They lined up in front of a lady wearing thick glasses. Joe and Sparky did, too.

"One, two, three — eyes on me!" said the lady. "Did everyone enjoy our field trip to Safari Land?"

"Yes, Miss Hootie," said the class.

As they answered, Miss Hootie cleaned her glasses. But *oops*! She dropped them. *CRACK!*

Then *oops*! She stepped on them. *CRUNCH!*

"Oh, dear!" said Miss Hootie, putting on her crooked, cracked glasses.

She squinted at Joe. "Is that you, Timmy?" she asked. "I thought you were absent today."

"That is not Timmy," said a boy. "That is a giraffe."

Miss Hootie looked closer. "Timmy, you are getting taller every day. And my, what a fun green hat!"

"That hat is a turtle," said a girl.

"Nonsense!" said Miss Hootie. "That is a hat if I ever saw one. You cannot pull one over on Miss Hootie here. Now, follow me. We still have half the school day left."

Miss Hootie turned around. She crashed into the bus.

"Oops! Pardon me," she said to the bus. "This way, kids. We will learn something new."

Everyone followed Miss Hootie. Joe did, too.

"No, Joe, no!" said Sparky. "I do not
want to learn something new. I want to go
home."

"Of course," said Joe. "After our field
trip to the school."

Inside, the class sat on a rug.

"Can anyone tell me what they learned today?" asked Miss Hootie.

"I learned that giraffes have twenty-inch tongues," said a boy.

Joe stuck out his tongue.

"And that they are taller than a bus!"
said another boy.

Joe stretched his neck.

"And that they go to school just like
us!" said a girl.

The class giggled.

"Simmer down," said Miss Hootie.
"Remember, good work gets a star."

She pointed to a sign:

BE A S.T.A.R.
Solve problems.
Try your best.
Always be kind.
Raise your hand.

Then Miss Hootie read a book. It was about Carl the Jolly Caterpillar.

"Never heard of him," said Sparky to Joe.

"Shh," said Joe.

"Caterpillars are delicious," said Sparky.

"BE QUIET!" said Joe.

"Timmy," said Miss Hootie, "if you must talk, please raise your hand."

But I do not have a hand, Joe thought.

After reading, Miss Hootie gave Sparky a star. "Good listening ears!" she said.

"Ears?" grumbled Joe. "What ears?" He wished he had a star, too.

Chapter Three
The Magic Pond

"Math time!" sang Miss Hootie. "Clap your hands. Stomp your feet. Put your bottoms in your seat!"

"I am beginning to wish I had hands," Joe said to Sparky.

"What is math?" Sparky asked.

"It must be that dance they just did," said Joe. "I will do the math, too."

Clap, clap! Stomp, stomp! CRASH!

Joe broke his chair.

Sparky hid in his shell. "Math is *very* dangerous."

Joe jumped up.

"OK," said Miss Hootie. "Everyone find a buddy."

"You will be my buddy," Joe said to Sparky. "I will work hard. I will get a star."

Miss Hootie gave each pair of buddies some peas to count.

"Oh, I see!" Sparky said to Joe. "Math is not a dance. Math is *food*."

Joe and Sparky ate 1, 2, 3, 4, 5, 6, 7, 8, 9, 10 peas.

"I am learning, Joe," said Sparky. "I am learning that the food is good here."

Miss Hootie checked on them. "How many peas do you have altogether?"

"BURP!" went Joe.

"Oh, dear!" said Miss Hootie. "No eating the math work, please!"

Joe still did not get a star.

"Bathroom break!" said Miss Hootie.
"Everyone follow me to the restrooms."

"Oh!" said Sparky. "A restroom sounds
like a wonderful place. After lunch, I like
to rest."

"Yes," said Joe. "We can nap there."

Everyone followed Miss
Hootie down the hall to
two doors. Joe and
Sparky looked at the
pictures on the doors.

"Where are the other doors?" asked Joe.

"Yes, where is the room for turtles?" asked Sparky.

"I do not see a room for giraffes, either," said Joe.

They walked into the boys' room.

"Well," said Joe. "This is not what I expected."

Sparky looked confused. "We can not nap here. Where is the pond? Where are the warm rocks?"

"This is not the best restroom," Joe agreed.

28

Sparky opened a door. "Oh! Here is a tiny pond!"

"What is this?" asked Joe, pressing a button.

WHOOSH!

Sparky gasped. The water was whirling away!

"Oh, no!" he cried. "Joe, what have you done? You made the pond disappear!"

Joe looked down. He looked worried.
He looked like he might cry.

"Wait, Joe!" said Sparky. "The pond!
It is coming back again."

Joe and Sparky whooped with joy.

"Do you know what we have learned,
Sparky?" asked Joe.

"What, Joe?"

"That schools have a magic pond," said
Joe.

Joe and Sparky made the magic pond
come and go, come and go.

WHOOSH! WHOOSH! WHOOSH!

Then Sparky took a shower . . .

Joe did his hair . . . and they tried
on a long scarf.

"We look great," said Joe.

Outside, the class was waiting for them.

"Did you wash your hands?" asked Miss Hootie.

Joe shook his head. "I do NOT have hands," he whispered to Sparky.

Miss Hootie frowned. "Please go wash your hands."

Joe still did not get a star.

Chapter Four
Who Is a S.T.A.R.?

For the rest of the day, Joe tried his best to get a star. He tried while feeding Rudy, the class pet . . . and at Music . . . and during a stretching break.

But to Joe's surprise, he had no luck.

Sparky was covered in stars. "I do not believe it. I have a learned a lot. I learned that I love school."

"Hmph," said Joe.

"Art time!" sang Miss Hootie. "Then we will go home."

"Oh, no!" said Joe. "I still do not have a star. I am almost out of time."

"Paint something you love," Miss Hootie told the class.

Sparky painted a picture.

Joe painted Sparky.

"Oh, mercy!" said Miss Hootie. "Do not paint your friends, please!"

Joe sighed. "That was my last chance. Now I will NEVER get a star!"

"Joe," said Sparky. "I have a surprise for you."

He showed Joe his painting.

"Sparky!" said Joe. "*You* gave me a star?"

"Yes," said Sparky. "You are a **S.T.A.R.** You **s**olved a problem when you got me off the bus. You **t**ried your best to listen to the story. You are **al**ways kind to me. And you would **r**aise your hand . . . if you had one."

Joe proudly hung the star around his neck.

Suddenly, *BRRRRRRRRIINNNNNG!*

"AGH!" Sparky jumped. "What was THAT?"

"The bell has rung," said Miss Hootie. "Good work today! Please line up for the bus."

Sparky hid in his shell. "Did she say b-b-b-bus?"

"Do not worry, my small, green friend," said Joe. "We will be walkers."

He lowered his head. Sparky climbed on. They headed home.

"School is cool," said Sparky.

"Next time," said Joe, "I will bring my pet worm, Wiggy, for Show-and-Tell."

Joe dropped Sparky off at his pond.

"Thank you for my star," said Joe.

On a nice warm rock, Sparky hid in his shell. ZZZZZZZZZ.

Not far away, Joe stretched his neck to see the world.